FRECKLE FACE

by

Neil Anderson

Illustrated by Barbara Cooney

"Freckle face, freckle face," Ann was called and she hated to be teased. Someone suggested the morning dew — another stump water to remove freckles. Then Ann read an advertisement about "Freckle Magic," but she had to earn $1.98 to pay for it. How did she do it? Did she have rose petals or freckles? Surprise!

*

Classification and Dewey Decimal: Easy (E)

About the Author:

NEIL ANDERSON is the penname for Jerrold Beim. He wrote his first story while in the fourth grade, and later, as a high school student, sold his first story to *Scholastic Magazine*. After graduating from high school he worked in a bank, as an office boy in an advertising department, and finally as advertising manager. Neil Anderson and his wife Lorraine lived in Mexico two years and it was there he started writing children's books.

About the Illustrator:

BARBARA COONEY and her twin brother were born in Brooklyn. Their mother was an artist, and Miss Cooney was fascinated by the tubes of paint, brushes and other artist's equipment always around the house. She was allowed to use these brushes and paints and so her career began. During World War II Miss Cooney joined the WACS. She has illustrated over fifty books and in 1959 received the Caldecott Medal.

FRECKLE FACE

FRECKLE FACE

By NEIL ANDERSON

Illustrated by Barbara Cooney

THIS SPECIAL EDITION IS PUBLISHED BY ARRANGEMENT WITH
THE PUBLISHERS OF THE REGULAR EDITION
THOMAS Y. CROWELL COMPANY
BY
E. M. HALE AND COMPANY
EAU CLAIRE, WISCONSIN

FRECKLE FACE

Ann lived on Maple Street. Her cousin Donny lived just around the corner. By cutting through their back yards they could get to each other's house right away.

Ann liked playing ball with Donny. She played cowboys and Indians with him, too.

But then she thought he ought to do something that she liked. "Let's play hop scotch," she said.

Donny shook his head. "No, I'd rather tie you up."

"I don't want to be tied up," Ann said. But Donny started to run around her with his rope.

"You're a baby!" Donny said.

"I am not! I'm two months older than you are." Ann pulled away.

"You're a baby and you're—you're a freckle face!" Donny laughed.

Donny knew that Ann hated being called "freckle face" more than anything in the world.

2

"Freckle face! Freckle face!" Donny said. "You have a hundred, thousand, million, billion, trillion freckles on your face!"

"I'm not going to play with you any more!" Ann said, and she ran into the house.

Ann looked at herself in the mirror. She had so many freckles in the winter and even more from the hot sun in the summer.

Mother came up to her. "Ann, what are you doing in the house? It's so nice outside."

"Oh, if I only didn't have these terrible freckles!" Ann said.

"I don't think they're terrible." Mother hugged Ann. "I think you are a beautiful little girl."

4

Ann felt a little better but she still
wished that she weren't such a freckle
face. She went outside again. Donny
was gone and she played with her girl
friends, June, Ruth, and Betty, instead.

6

Ann thought her friend June was so
pretty. Someone once said that June had
skin just like rose petals. None of her
friends had freckles. Ann wished she were
as pretty as the other girls.

The next Saturday morning Ann went to the grocery store for her mother. She had to wait her turn and she saw herself in the glass showcase.

"Why are you looking so sad this morning?" Mr. Fred, the grocery store man, asked her.

"Freckles!" Ann said. "I just wish I didn't have all these freckles!"

"I think they're nice," Mr. Fred said. "But I once heard how you can make them go away."

"You did!" Ann exclaimed. "How can I do it?"

"Well, you're supposed to get up early in the morning and gather the dew off the grass," Mr. Fred said. "Then you wash your face with the dew and your freckles will disappear."

8

Ann could hardly sleep that night, waiting for morning to come. It would be wonderful if Donny could never call her "freckle face" again.

When the sun came up, Ann got out of bed. She tiptoed out of the house and gathered dew off the grass. How soft and cool it felt against her face. If only it would make her freckles go away!

10

Ann waited and waited all day. She kept running to the mirror. At first she thought she had a few less freckles. Maybe it was working.

She looked and looked but finally she had to admit that nothing was happening at all.

Ann felt terrible. She didn't even want to play with June, Ruth, or Betty. Instead she went to visit Carol who was only two years old and lived in the house next door.

Ann thought Carol was a darling baby. She had such curly hair and pretty blue eyes and not a freckle on her face.

"My goodness, you look sad today," Carol's mother said. "Is anything the matter?"

"Oh, I just wish I didn't have all these freckles!" Ann said.

Carol's mother smiled. "My grandmother once told me of a way to get rid of freckles. You wash your face with rain water from an old oak stump. But I don't know if it really works—"

"I'll try it!" Ann said.

Ann found an old oak stump but
there wasn't any rain water in it. She
waited and waited and one day it finally
rained. She ran to the oak stump and
washed her face with rain water.

How soft and cool it felt against her
face! If only it would make her freckles
go away!

14

But when Ann looked in the mirror, she had as many freckles as ever.

"Freckle face! Freckle face!" Donny teased her the next time they played together.

That very afternoon Ann was at home stretched out on the floor, looking at a magazine. She turned a page and her eyes grew wide at what she saw.

Freckle Magic
Get Rid of Your Freckles
Only $1.98

Ann showed it to her mother. "Could I buy it? Could we send for it?" she asked.

"No, Ann," Mother said. "It would just be throwing money away. I don't believe it really works. Besides, I like your freckles."

16

Ann still wanted to send away for the Freckle Magic. She had a little bit of money saved up but not enough. She walked down the street wondering how she could ever get a dollar ninety-eight.

Snip-snip-snip! Ann heard a sound and then she saw a neighbor, Mr. Rand, working in his garden. Mr. Rand had such a beautiful garden.

18

"I'm not as young as I used to be," Mr. Rand said as he got up. "I ought to hire someone to help me with this work."

"I could help you," Ann said. "I need money badly—to buy something."

"Well, why don't you start right now?" Mr. Rand said, handing Ann his clippers.

Snip—snip—snip! Ann loved working in the garden among the beautiful flowers. She worked part of that afternoon and part of the next afternoon, too.

"How much do I owe you?" Mr. Rand asked Ann when she finished.

"I don't know," Ann said.

Mr. Rand looked at Ann. "Well, why don't we say I'll pay you a penny for every freckle on your face? You count them when you get home and I'll give you the money tomorrow."

For once Ann didn't mind looking in the mirror. She counted her freckles before she went to bed that night.

One—two—three—up to fifty-six—fifty-seven—until a hundred and sixty-one. She needed only a few more cents for the Freckle Magic.

22

Ann didn't go to see Mr. Rand until the next afternoon. Before lunch she lay on the grass in the sun waiting for more freckles to come.

Then Ann went to see Mr. Rand.

"I have one hundred and sixty-three freckles," Ann said. "I lay in the sun to get some more."

Mr. Rand smiled. "What are you going to do with the money?" he asked.

"Buy Freckle Magic to get rid of my freckles," Ann said. "I tried dew from the grass but it didn't work. I tried rain water from an old oak stump but it didn't work. Freckle Magic sounds as if it will really make them go away."

"I wouldn't count on it too much," Mr. Rand said as he gave Ann the money.

Ann sent away for the Freckle Magic. And one day it finally came. She opened the package and there was a small bottle. She read what it said on the bottle and then rubbed the white Freckle Magic all over her face.

Oh, how it hurt! It burned and it stung. She thought her skin was coming right off!

It felt so terrible that Ann knew the Freckle Magic must be working. She went to the mirror to see.

Her face looked as white as a clown's.

She watched the clock. After five minutes she carefully washed off the Freckle Magic.

She looked in the mirror again. All her freckles were still there.

It wasn't magic at all!

24

Donny came over to Ann's house the next morning.

"Come on, Ann, let's play," he said. "Let's be pioneers and go across the country in a covered wagon. And then the Indians will come—"

"And then you'll want to scalp me," Ann said. "No thank you! I think I'll go over to Mr. Rand's garden."

Donny walked along beside Ann. "What are you going to go over there for?" he asked.

"I help him in his garden," Ann said.

"Does he pay you for it? Or do you do it just for fun?" Donny asked.

Ann was glad that they reached the garden just then. She didn't want Donny to know that Mr. Rand had paid her by the freckles on her face!

26

"Good morning," Mr. Rand said. "I was wondering if my helper was coming along today. I can use you—"

"Can you use me, too?" Donny put in.

"Why yes, of course," Mr. Rand said. "Why don't you pull some of the weeds out here and Ann can clip over there."

Donny was such a good help that, for a while, Ann didn't mind that he had come along. But when they were done, Mr. Rand asked, "Well, how should I pay you today, Ann?"

She was afraid that Mr. Rand was going to say that he would pay her for each freckle! She looked around and then she exclaimed, "Could I have a bouquet of flowers from your garden? I love them!"

"Of course you may have flowers from my garden," Mr. Rand said to Ann. Then he turned to Donny. "Do you want the same thing?"

"Well, yes, my mother would like some flowers," Donny said.

"Then let's go around the garden and you can pick out the ones you want." Mr. Rand started to lead the way.

Ann and Donny walked around the garden. "I'd like some of these." Ann pointed to the roses. "And some of these, and maybe some of these, too." She chose other flowers.

"I'll take the same," Donny said. "Oh, I like those, too! They're tiger lilies, aren't they? I used to see them when I went to a farm one summer. They're my favorite flower."

28

Ann leaned forward to look at the tiger lilies. "Why, Mr. Rand!" she exclaimed, "the tiger lilies—they have little spots all over them. Just like freckles—"

"Yes, they do," Mr. Rand said. "Some of the most beautiful flowers have freckles on them. Look at these pansies —they have freckles. And those white lilies.

"I guess that's why people often say that little girls look like pretty flowers."

Ann and Donny thanked Mr. Rand for their flowers and they started for home.

Ann looked at the tiger lilies and then she looked at Donny.

"Why do you always call me freckle face, if you really like—freckle faces?" Ann asked.

"Oh, because I know it always makes you mad." Donny grinned. "I really like your freckles—"

Just then June, Ruth, and Betty came along.

"Oh, what beautiful flowers you have! Where did you get them?" June asked.

"Mr. Rand gave them to me for helping in his garden," Ann said.

"Are you lucky!" Betty exclaimed.

"I know," said Ann. She looked again at the flowers. She not only felt lucky. She suddenly felt pretty, too. As pretty as a flower in a bouquet.